WS

The Monster
and the Teddy Bear

For Callum, Eva and Chloë

Copyright © 1989 by David McKee

The rights of David McKee to be identified as the author and illustrator of this work have
been asserted by him in accordance with the Copyright, Designs and Patents Act, 1988.
First published in Great Britain in 1989 by Andersen Press Ltd., 20 Vauxhall Bridge Road,
London SW1V 2SA.
This paperback edition first published in 1997 by Andersen Press Ltd.
Published in Australia by Random House Australia Pty., 20 Alfred Street, Milsons Point,
Sydney, NSW 2061. All rights reserved. Colour separated in Switzerland by Photolitho AG,
Offsetreproduktionen, Gossau, Zürich. Printed and bound in Italy by Grafiche AZ, Verona.

10   9   8   7   6   5   4   3   2

British Library Cataloguing in Publication Data available.

ISBN 0 86264 762 2

This book has been printed on acid-free paper

The Monster
and the Teddy Bear

David McKee

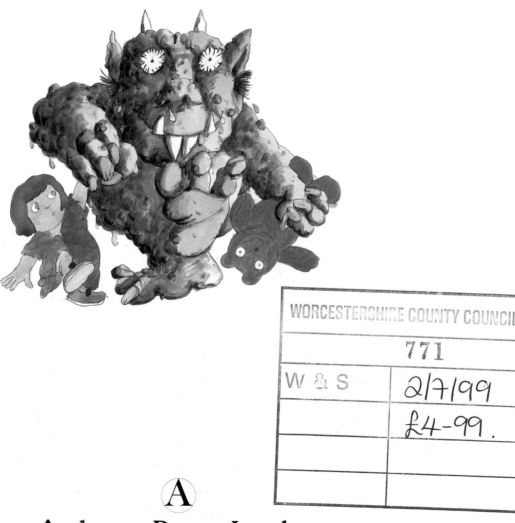

Ⓐ

Andersen Press · London

"Aunt Jane has sent you a teddy bear," said Angela's mother.
"I don't like teddy bears," said Angela. "I want a monster."

"Everyone likes teddy bears," said Mother. "They're warm and cuddly."
"And monsters are big and strong and exciting," said Angela.
"I want a monster."

That evening Mummy and Daddy went out. Angela went to bed and the babysitter sat in front of the television.

Suddenly, there at Angela's window, was a monster.
"Hello, Angela," said the monster. "I'm your monster."
"Great!" said Angela. "But what a smell!" she thought.

"Who's that?" said the monster as he bounced over the bed.
"Oh, that's just boring old teddy," laughed Angela.

"He can come with us while we do monstrous things,"
said the monster.
"Oh goody, monstrous things!" said Angela.

"First I want to eat," said the monster.
Angela shuddered when she felt the monster's slimy hand.
"Still it is a monster's hand," she thought. The monster
stomped downstairs.

"Angela, be quiet!" shouted the babysitter and she turned the
television louder.

In the kitchen the monster emptied the fridge and cupboards.

He made monstrous sandwiches and ate everything,
even the flowers.

After he'd finished eating the monster found some paint under the sink and started to redecorate the kitchen.

Then he gave a huge BURRRRP!

"Angela, be quiet!" shouted the babysitter as she turned up the television again.

"What a mess!" said Angela.
"You call that a mess?" said the monster. "Wait until we start doing monstrous things!"
"You're horrible," said Angela. "What will Mummy and Daddy say?"

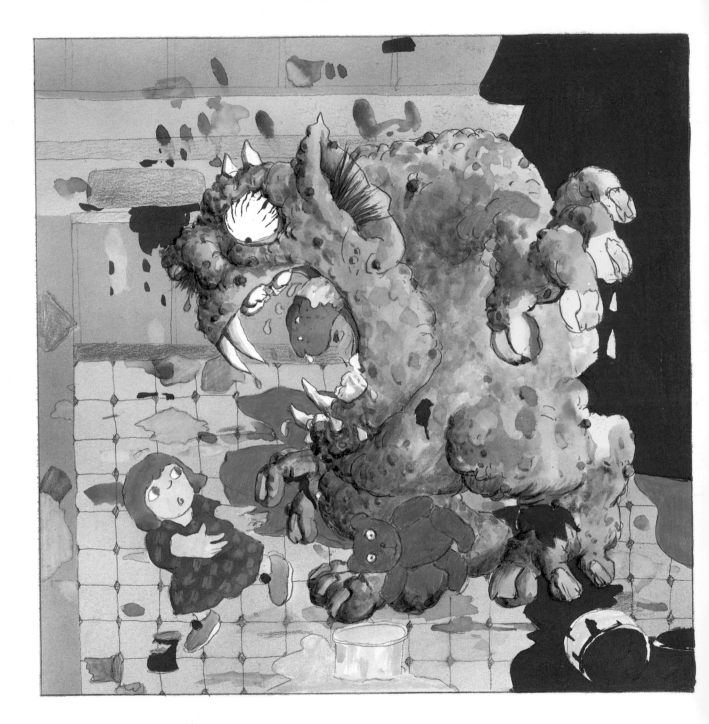

"Nothing!" roared the monster. "Or I'll eat them, and if you start moaning I'll eat you as well. Monsters can do anything."

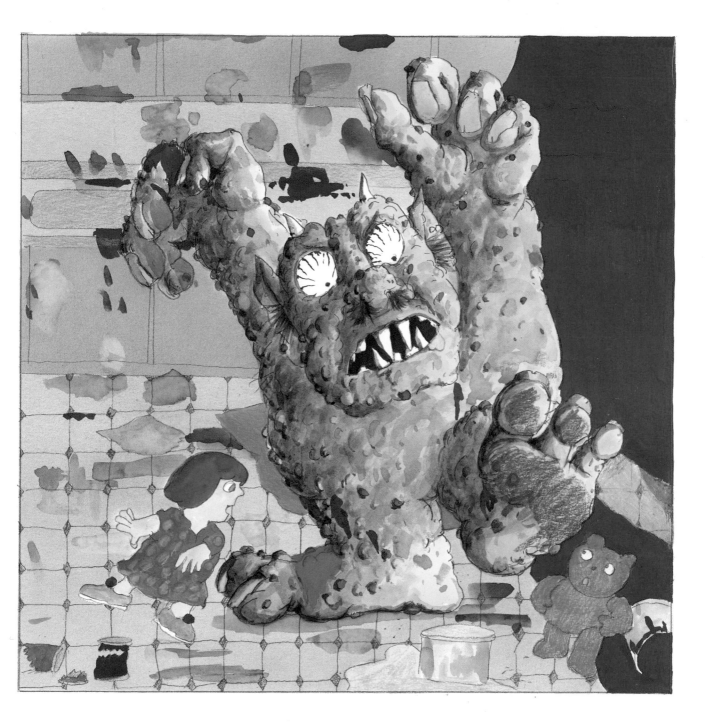

"No, they can't," said Teddy. "They can't be warm and
cuddly."

"And you can't be a monster, boring old Teddy Bear," snarled the monster. "I'm going to throw you so far you'll never come back."

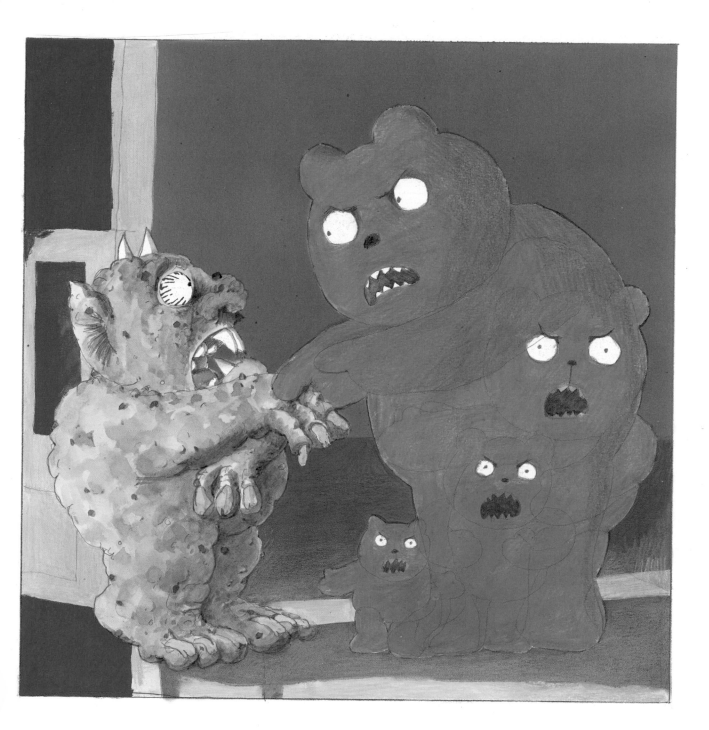

"You'll what?" said Teddy. "You'll what?" And he growled, and as he growled he grew. "It's *me* that's going to throw *you* so far that *you'll* never come back," he said.

Still growling he dragged the monster out into the garden.

Outside in the garden Teddy spun the monster round and round above his head.

With a roar he threw the monster and he threw him so far that
for sure he'd never come back.

"ANGELA!" shouted the babysitter.

"You were wonderful," said Angela as Teddy became himself again. "But what will Mummy and Daddy say?"

"Come on. Let's go back to bed," said Teddy. "Perhaps they'll never notice."

More Andersen Press paperback picture books!

OUR PUPPY'S HOLIDAY
by Ruth Brown

SCRATCH 'N' SNIFF
by Gus Clarke

FRIGHTENED FRED
by Peta Coplans

I HATE MY TEDDY BEAR
by David McKee

THE HILL AND THE ROCK
by David McKee

MR UNDERBED
by Chris Riddell

WHAT DO YOU WANT TO BE, BRIAN?
by Jeanne Willis and Mary Rees

MICHAEL
by Tony Bradman and Tony Ross

THE LONG BLUE BLAZER
by Jeanne Willis and Susan Varley

FROG IS A HERO
by Max Velthuijs